Tania started writing poetry and short stories at a very young age. Her work has won numerous awards and prizes. She continued excelling in written art at Johns Hopkins University. After spending several years raising her two toddlers, *King Crumble Won't Sleep* is her first exciting adventure in the world of publication. She currently lives in Baltimore.

AUSTIN MACAULEY PUBLISHERS™
LONDON • CAMBRIDGE • NEW YORK • SHARJAH
TANIA HABIB
KING CRUMBLE
WON'T SLEEP

Copyright © Tania Habib (2020)

Ordering Information:
Quantity sales: special discounts are available on quantity purchases by corporations, associations, and others. For details, contact the publisher at the address below.

Publisher's Cataloging-in-Publication data
Habib, Tania
King Crumble Won't Sleep

ISBN 9781647504700 (Paperback)
ISBN 9781647504694 (Hardback)
ISBN 9781647504717 (ePub e-book)
ISBN 9781647504687 (Audiobook)

Library of Congress Control Number: 2020918106

www.austinmacauley.com/us

First Published (2020)
Austin Macauley Publishers LLC
40 Wall Street, 28th Floor
New York, NY 10005
USA

mail-usa@austinmacauley.com
+1 (646) 5125767

To my family, the nuttiest but sweetest batch of cookies I know.

King Crumble was not a very sweet treat;
he wasn't a cookie that you'd want to eat.
He didn't like bathing or scrubbing his toes,
and said that the bubbles tickled his nose.

He didn't like sharing or passing the ball.
Some said that this cookie
liked nothing at all.
What he disliked the most was
bedtime at night.
"I won't sleep!" he yelled as he
switched on the light.
He threw up his arms and stomped
on the ground,
yelling and making a terrible sound!
He sat on the floor and
he stubbornly stewed,
a crumby ol' king in a crumby ol' mood.

One late Friday night, while the
world was in bed,
a brilliant idea entered
King Crumble's head.
With a smile on his face,
he stood up real tall,
"I'll get rid of bedtime,
once and for all!"

He gathered together the
cookies he knew:
the wafers and shortbreads and
macaroons too.
He told them to each stay
awake by his side.
"'Cause sleeping is silly!"
the grumpy king cried.

"Toss your pillows away,"
the loud cookie said,
"for we will not EVER go back to bed!"
They picked up their forks and
wielded their spoons,
aiming their cutlery straight
at the moon.

"We'll stay up all night until
morning is here,
and sleep will not ever dare to come
near!"
They all stood around as stars
filled up the skies.
Some started to yawn while
rubbing their eyes.

Some reached for their blankets
and one for his teddy,
even though nobody felt they were
ready.
Soon you could hear nothing,
not even a peep...
for even King Crumble was fast,
fast asleep.

9 781647 504694